I LOVE YOU,
BLUE

BARROUX

I HAVE ALWAYS LOVED THE BLUE OF THE OCEAN.

THE SMELL OF THE WIND, THE CALM....

BUT TODAY THE SKY TURNS BLACK.

THE SEA ROARS AND RAGES.

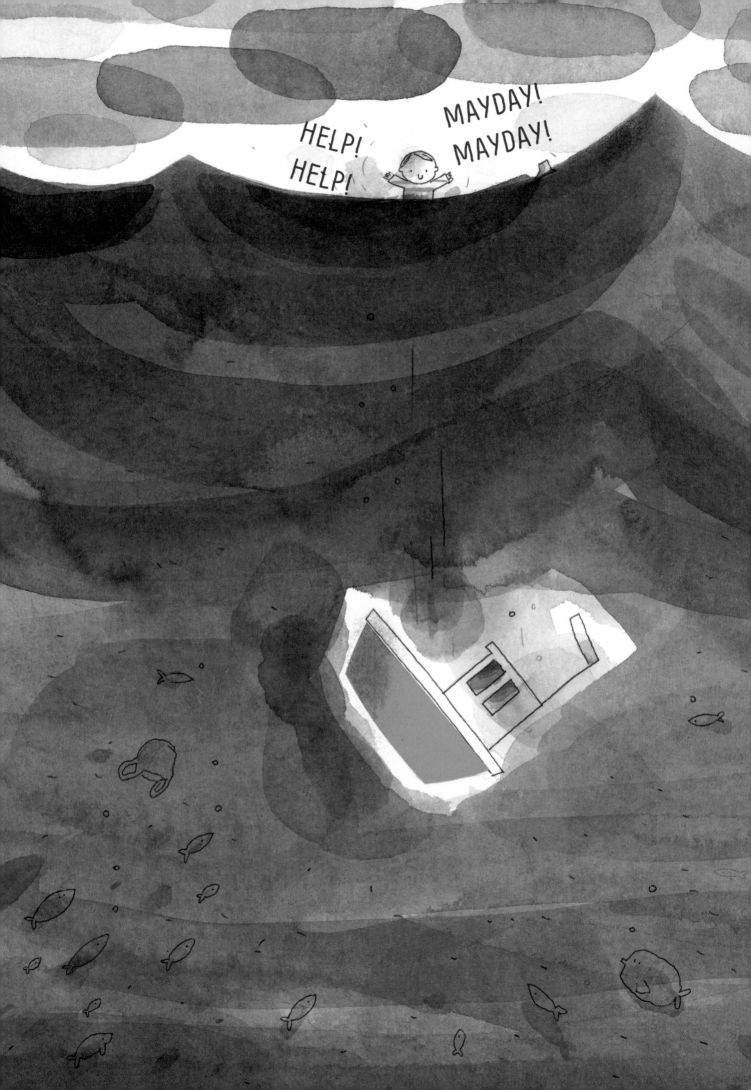

THANK YOU!
THANK YOU SO MUCH.
YOU SAVED MY LIFE.

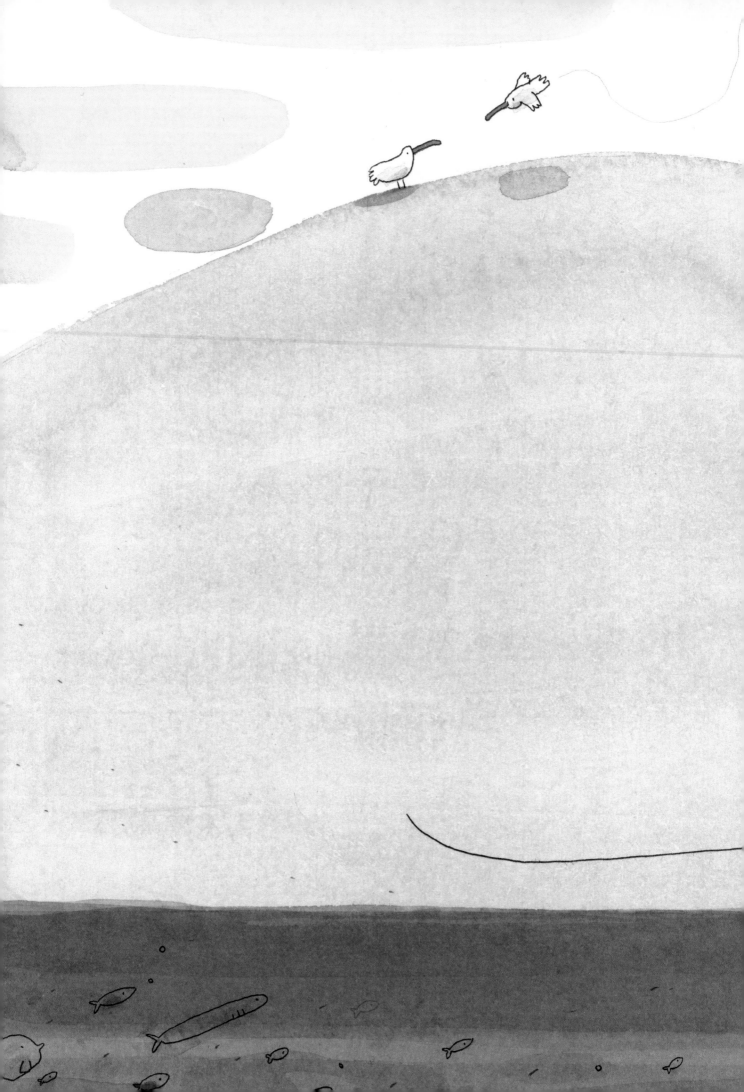

MY NAME IS JONAS, WHAT'S YOURS?

BLUE.

BLUE, THANK YOU AGAIN.
YOU ARE SO BEAUTIFUL.
I HOPE I WILL SEE YOU TOMORROW.

BLUE, BLUE...
YOU ARE THE PRETTIEST OF WHALES.

BLUE, BLUE...

GOOD NIGHT.

TRA LA LA! IT'S A LOVELY DAY.

HERE I COME, BLUE!

NO ONE! NOTHING!

HAS SOMETHING HAPPENED?

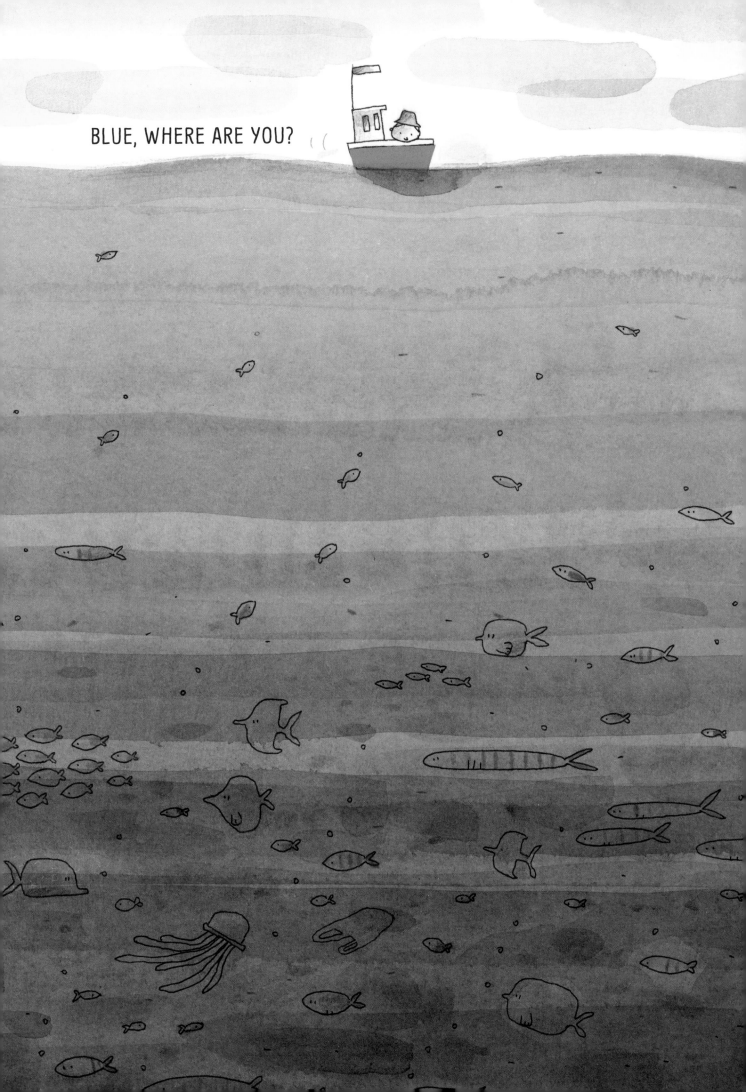

BLUE, WHERE ARE YOU?

OH, BLUE, THERE YOU ARE!

YOU LOOK TERRIBLE.
ARE YOU ILL?
OPEN YOUR MOUTH, SAY "AAAAH!"

WOW! IT'S HUGE IN HERE.

POOR BLUE!
NO WONDER YOU'RE SICK.
YOU HAVE A BELLY FULL OF PLASTIC BAGS!

LET'S GET RID OF ALL THIS RUBBISH.
THEN YOU WILL FEEL MUCH BETTER.

I'M TAKING ALL THESE PLASTIC BAGS AWAY.
JELLYFISH ARE A MUCH BETTER BREAKFAST
FOR YOU, BLUE.

HAVE A GOOD REST AND I'LL SEE YOU TOMORROW.

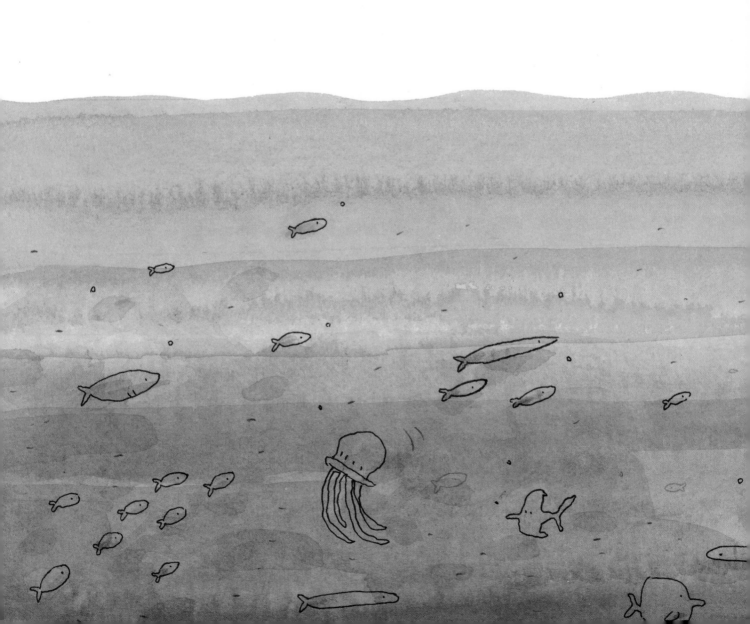

BUT THE NEXT DAY...

NO ONE.

NOTHING.

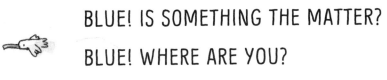

BLUE! IS SOMETHING THE MATTER?

BLUE! WHERE ARE YOU?

BLUE?

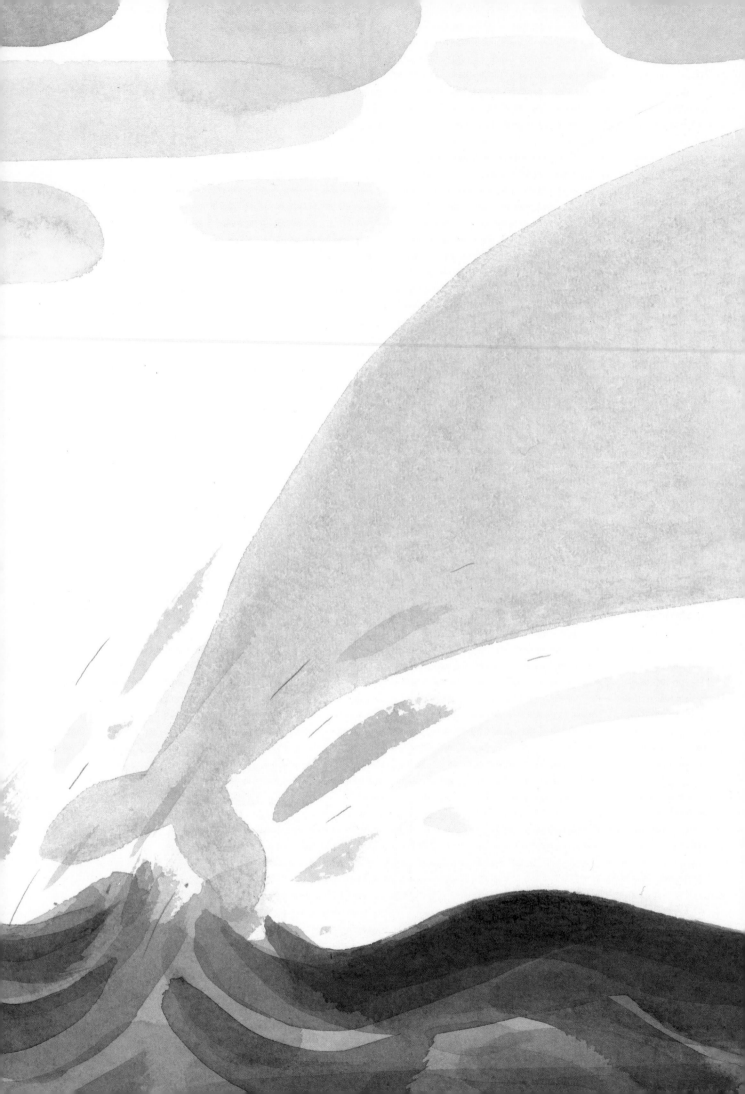

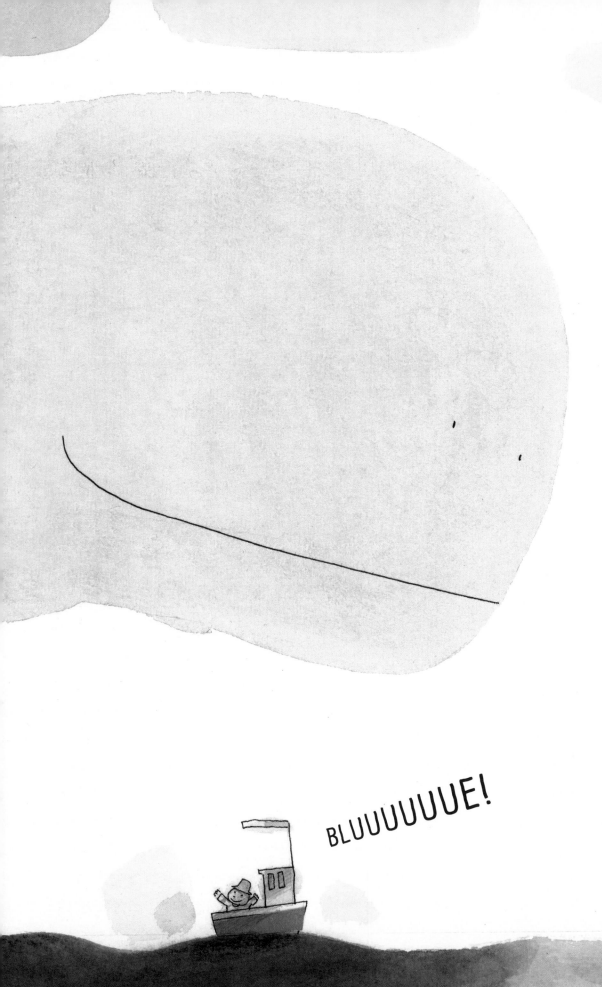

I LOVE YOU, BLUE.

SAVE OUR OCEANS.
SAVE OUR WHALES.

SAVE OUR OCEANS, SAVE OUR WHALES
A MESSAGE FROM BARROUX

In my story Blue stands for every kind of whale – over 20 different species. Many of them are in danger of extinction. Some are protected by international laws or agreements, but they all face a constant new danger – plastic pollution. Even Blue Whales, which strain their food through a mesh inside their mouths, swallow vast amounts of tiny plastic particles. Others, like Sperm Whales and Grey Whales, swallow whole plastic bags, thinking they are food. All can be killed by the build-up of plastic in their stomachs. Huge amounts of plastic waste are dumped in the sea every day.

To protect whales and all sea life, we must stop polluting our oceans. Here are five ways you can help:

- ◆ Don't use plastic bags unless they are recyclable or compostable.
- ◆ Don't use plastic bottles. They can take 450 years to decompose.
- ◆ Don't use throwaway plastic items like cups and straws.
- ◆ Only buy things wrapped in plastic if the plastic can be recycled.
- ◆ Go on a beach clean-up with your family and friends.

To find out more about how to protect whales go to –

WDC (Whale & Dolphin Conservation) – a global charity with its own site for children: **www.wdcs.org/wdcskids**

Save the Whales – a California-based charity focused on what young people can do: **www.savethewhales.org**